George Washington Carver

by **Mary Taylor**
illustrated by **Leah Palmer**

HOUGHTON MIFFLIN   BOSTON

A lot of people love to eat peanut butter.
But not everyone knows where it first came from.
Peanut butter was invented by an African American
scientist named George Washington Carver.

When George was little, he lived on a farm where everybody had to work hard. But George was sick a lot so he wasn't strong enough to help with most of the hard work.

George worked around the house while his brother Jim worked in the fields. George learned to cook and clean. He also learned to read and play the fiddle. But the thing he liked to do the best was explore outdoors.

When he was a child, George grew his own garden. He used seeds he got from flowers in the woods and fields. He knew how to take care of sick plants too. People who knew George called him the "plant doctor."

George wanted to learn all about the world.
"I wanted to know every strange stone,
flower, insect, bird, or beast," he once wrote. But
there was no one nearby that he could learn from.

George left home when he was 12. He moved to a town where he could go to school. At school he learned about plants. He also learned about art.

George went to college to study art when he was old enough. He was a good artist. But his art teacher saw that George knew about plants too. The teacher thought George should go to a different college to learn science. So George changed schools.

George learned a lot about science and about plants. After a few years at the college, he became a teacher.

George became a very good scientist. Soon a college in the South asked him to teach. It was a new college for African American students.

George liked being a teacher. He remembered that when he was growing up there were not many schools that African Americans could go to. Now George could help other African Americans learn.

While George was teaching he heard that many farmers in the South were having a hard time. Most of them grew cotton. Cotton plants are not good for the soil. The cotton made the land too poor for growing most things.

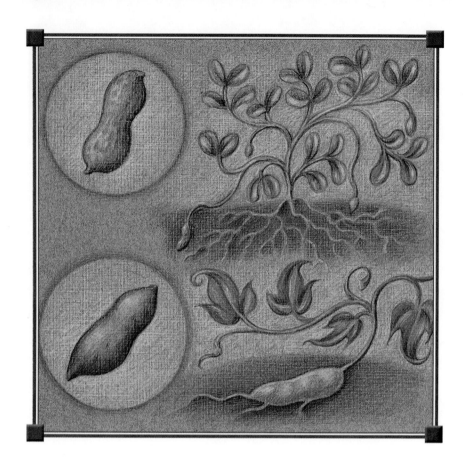

George taught farmers that some plants, such as peanuts and sweet potatoes, could make the soil rich again. So he began to show farmers how to grow these crops.

George told farmers to plant peanuts one year and cotton the next year. This kept the soil rich and farmers were able to grow bigger and better crops.

But soon there was another problem. The farmers grew so many peanuts they couldn't sell them all. So George invented new ways to use peanuts.

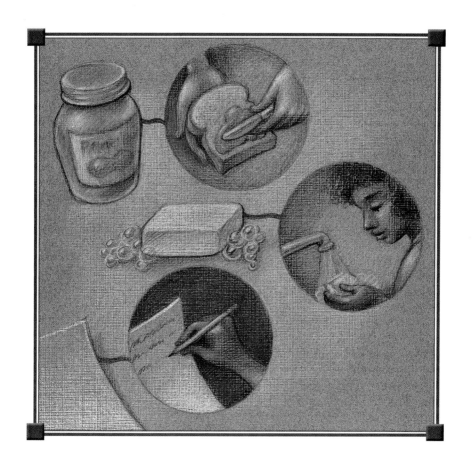

George used every part of the peanut plant in his inventions. He made paper from peanut vines and skins. He used peanuts to make soap and shampoo. George also made over 100 kinds of foods from peanuts—including peanut butter!

George Washington Carver was smart and he was kind. He knew a lot about science. And he used what he learned to help people have better lives.